Magical Hair

Vanessa Hammonds

To order additional copies of this book, contact:
Xlibris
844-714-8691
www.Xlibris.com
Orders@Xlibris.com

ISBN: Softcover   978-1-6698-1318-7
        EBook   978-1-6698-1317-0

Print information available on the last page

Rev. date: 02/22/2022

"*Magical Hair*"

Vanessa Hammonds

MY name is Zhi and I love being me. My hair is big and as curly as can be.

Or sometimes its short... or even a buzzed cut!
I choose my hairstyles by listening to my gut.

My hair always makes me shine. I change it up so much, it can go from curly to straight in Days' time

Whether its long, short, half shaved... I always feel so brave! I enjoy trying out new styles because every time I change it up it makes me smile.

I can wear it in braids, puffs, in an afro or in locs,. The possibilities of my hairstyle choices never stop!

My hair is just magical, don't you see. I am not my hair but my hair is me.

Printed in the United States
by Baker & Taylor Publisher Services